Five Seconds

Story by Nicolas Brasch
Illustrations by Jeff Crowther

Five Seconds

Text: Nicolas Brasch
Publishers: Tania Mazzeo and Eliza Webb
Series consultant: Amanda Sutera
Hands on Heads Consulting
Editor: Jess Mackay
Project editor: Annabel Smith
Designer: Jess Kelly
Project designer: Danielle Maccarone
Illustrations: Jeff Crowther
Production controller: Renee Tome

NovaStar

ISBN 978 0 17 033479 2

Cengage Learning Australia
Level 5, 80 Dorcas Street
Southbank VIC 3006 Australia
Phone: 1300 790 853
Email: aust.nelsonprimary@cengage.com

For learning solutions, visit **cengage.com.au**

Printed in China by 1010 Printing International Ltd
1 2 3 4 5 6 7 29 28 27 26 25

Nelson acknowledges the Traditional Owners and Custodians of the lands of all First Nations Peoples. We pay respect to Elders past and present, and extend that respect to all First Nations Peoples today.

Contents

	Author Warning	5
Chapter 1	Black Holes	6
Chapter 2	The Spade	11
Chapter 3	Thunder and Lightning	15
Chapter 4	The Penalty	19
Chapter 5	Wide Awake	26
Chapter 6	The Guessing Game	30
Chapter 7	The Surprise Party	36
Chapter 8	Time Vanishes	42

Author Warning

The main character in this story digs a large hole in his back garden using heavy, sometimes dangerous, tools. Do not do this at home. I mean, do not do this in your garden if you have one. (If you do it in your home you won't get far; the floor is probably much too strong to dig through. And if the floor isn't that strong, you need to move house.)

So, do not do what the main character in this story does. It may be dangerous, you might get hurt, and you'll almost certainly ruin the garden. Most importantly, it's very, very hard work and you'll just end up with a mess (or maybe hit underground electrical cables and water pipes).

Chapter 1

Black Holes

Today, I woke up before the sunrise to finish reading a book about a time traveller who went back to when dinosaurs roamed Earth. I then had to spend the day at school – how boring in comparison – but I returned home and started a new book about a time traveller going back to ancient Rome.

That got me thinking. I wish there really was a way to time travel.

The next morning, I was still thinking about travelling back in time – where I could go, what I could do. I was so deep in thought that while leaving the house, I almost tripped over a spade lying in the front garden. Dad must have left it there after he finished planting a new tree yesterday afternoon.

My next-door neighbour and best friend, Eve, was waiting for me at my front gate. We walked to school together, like we always did.

The first class was maths, and we were learning about fractions. Who cares about fractions? My mind quickly wandered.

Next up was science.

"Does anyone know what a black hole is?" asked our teacher, Ms Redondo.

None of us answered.

"You were right not to raise your hands," Ms Redondo said, "because even scientists aren't sure what black holes are. Though some believe that if time travel was possible ..."

My ears pricked up.

Ms Redondo continued, "... then it could only happen if you were sucked into one."

What? Really? My brain started buzzing. So, time travel might *actually* be possible?

Ms Redondo went on to explain that black holes are in space and inside these black holes are things called wormholes. And that these wormholes might be tunnels into the past.

She also said, “Scientists often try things that everyone else thinks are impossible. The scientists are frequently wrong, but when they’re right, they can change the world.”

Although I stayed at school physically for the rest of the day, my mind was somewhere else. In space to be exact. In black holes and wormholes and the past.

Chapter 2

The Spade

On the way home, I said to Eve, "Wouldn't it be awesome to have our own black hole and be able to time travel?"

"It's not possible, Oliver," she said.

"I know that. I'm just saying."

"They're billions of light years away. In space."

"I know."

There was no point continuing this chat. Eve just didn't want to even imagine it.

I mumbled goodbye to her as I walked through my front gate and up the path.

"Ow!" This time I tripped over Dad's spade and fell onto the ground.

But as I grabbed the spade to toss it aside, I had a wild thought.

If time travel was possible through a wormhole, and wormholes existed in black holes, then all I needed was a black hole with worms. After all, worms wriggle through tunnels.

My mind raced on. If I dug a hole deep into the ground, and I found a wormhole big enough to crawl through, who knows what might happen?

Okay, the idea was wild. So very, very wild. But according to Ms Redondo, this could be my chance to change the world.

I grabbed the spade, took it into the back garden and picked a spot around the corner from the kitchen window, so Mum and Dad wouldn't see me. They were very proud of their garden and a huge hole wouldn't be part of their landscaping.

I struck the blade of the spade into the ground. Luckily it had been raining recently, and the ground wasn't too hard. I started digging and before long, the mound of dirt from my hole grew and grew.

I dug and dug.

At one point, Eve looked over the fence and asked what I was doing. I told her I was digging a hole.

"I can see that," she said. "But why?"

"Come and help me and I'll tell you."

So she did. I handed her my spade so I could have a rest. As she dug, I outlined my plan about digging a black hole, finding a wormhole, crawling through a worm tunnel and travelling back in time.

"That's the most ridiculous thing I have ever heard," she said.

And she handed me back the spade and went home.

Chapter 3

Thunder and Lightning

I dug until it was almost dark. The hole was already big enough for me to stand in. But I wanted it deeper, much deeper.

"Dinner time, Oliver!" I heard Dad bellow from the back door.

The next thing I saw was his head looking down at me from above the hole.

"What on Earth is this? What's going on here?" Dad asked.

"I … I … I …"

I didn't know what to say.

"It's sort of a science project," I told him.

"Then I need to talk to your teacher," Dad said sternly.

"No. Please, no."

Okay, the truth was needed. “I think I might know how to time travel,” I blurted out.

“Time travel? Are you joking? You’re obsessed with it!” replied Dad, looking completely baffled. “It’s too dark now, but straight after school tomorrow I want you to start filling this hole. Come in and clean up for dinner.” And he turned and walked back to the house.

At that moment, black clouds slid across the sky. There was a boom of thunder and torrential rain started falling. Suddenly, there was a flash of lightning and the loudest thunderclap I had ever heard. It scared the life out of me.

Mum opened the back door and yelled at me to hurry inside. I took a step towards the house but slipped backwards. I grabbed the spade for support, but it wasn't much help. I toppled back into the hole, the spade still in my hand.

I landed on my back, shaken but unhurt.

Another bolt of lightning flashed from the sky, and the end of it hit the metal blade of the spade.

A mild electric shock ran through me and I let go of the spade's wooden handle, which now had scorch marks on it. I climbed out of the hole and went inside to clean up for dinner.

That night, I had the most restless sleep I've ever had.

Chapter 4

The Penalty

The next morning, the sun was out. It was as if the storm had never happened. That was both good news and bad news. Good news because it was sports day, and I would get to play soccer for the school. Bad news because I would have to start filling in the hole when I got home.

I slowly got out of bed and took my time getting ready before heading to school.

We were playing soccer against our biggest rivals, the team from the school on the other side of the highway. Their nickname was "the Eagles".

It was a semi-final, and we were desperate to win. We had never played in a final before. The problem was the Eagles hadn't missed a final for five years. They took their soccer very seriously.

That afternoon, our coach, Ms McElroy, handed out our soccer shirts, gave us a pep talk and then announced the positions we would play. I would be striker. I didn't usually play striker, but today it was my job to score goals. So much pressure!

I started the game full of nerves but as the match went on, I relaxed and enjoyed myself. With one minute to go in the match, the score was still 0–0.

It looked like the match would go to extra time. If so, we were done for. We were exhausted, and the Eagles seemed like they had more energy than us.

Then, as we had one last attempt at goal, the ball bounced off a clump of grass and hit the hand of one of the Eagles' players – definitely against the rules.

The referee blew her whistle and awarded us a penalty – a free shot at goal that only the goalkeeper could try to save. And as the striker, I would be the one to take it!

I placed the ball on the spot and took five steps back. I stared at the goalkeeper, who stared straight back at me. My teammates started chanting my name.

"Oliver! Oliver! Oliver!"

I took a deep breath, ran up to the ball and hit it sweetly with my right foot towards the goalkeeper's right. Unfortunately, she dived to her right and caught the ball.

I dropped my head into my hands. I was so disappointed. I had let my teammates down. I felt the tears well up inside me. I closed my eyes and suddenly, I had a vision of the black hole I had dug. I wanted to jump into it and disappear.

Then, the strangest thing *ever* happened. As the image of the hole burned in my mind, I felt a tingling through my body, a bit like an electric shock.

Something incredible had happened. I was lining up to take the penalty. Again!

My teammates were chanting my name again. It was as if I had not yet taken the penalty. It was as if I had gone back in time by five seconds. And so had everyone else.

My whole world had gone back five seconds.

I stared at the goalkeeper, who stared straight back at me. I took a deep breath and ran towards the ball. I already knew she was going to dive to the right, so I kicked it towards her left.

Goal!

My teammates ran towards me. They embraced me and jumped all over me. I was a hero.

Chapter 5

Wide Awake

When school finished, Eve was waiting for me at the gate to walk home together.

"I heard about the goal!" she said. "Everyone was talking about it. You're a star!"

"Thanks," I said, but I didn't sound happy. I was so confused.

"I thought you'd be excited," Eve said.

I shook my head.

"What's up?" she asked.

If there was one person who I could talk to about what happened, it was Eve. We shared everything.

I took a deep breath and started telling Eve what had happened. By the time I'd finished explaining, we had walked all the way back home. Eve was shaking her head.

"Impossible," she said.

"I know. But it happened."

"Are you telling me that because of the black hole you dug, you somehow travelled back in time by five seconds?"

"Exactly."

She shook her head. "But why only five seconds?"

"That's what I have to figure out."

I didn't fill the hole back in that afternoon. When Dad got home and asked about it, I told him I had too much homework to do.

"Tomorrow," he insisted.

I couldn't get to sleep that night. I was too busy wondering if I had really travelled back in time or just imagined it. I replayed the penalties over and over in my mind. Maybe I had imagined missing the first one and only the second one was real.

And if I had travelled in time, why only five seconds? Why not back to another time in history? Maybe the hole in the garden could help me figure things out.

When I knew Mum and Dad were asleep, I got out of bed, grabbed a torch, crept outside and stood above the hole. I couldn't see anything unusual about the hole. And it wasn't that big. Not compared to a *real* black hole.

That's it! I thought. A black hole is enormous. If you can travel back in time by thousands or even millions of years through a black hole, then a hole the fraction of that size would allow you to travel back a fraction of that time. Like five seconds.

Maybe fractions are useful to learn after all.

Chapter 6

The Guessing Game

School the following day started with a history lesson. I was sitting next to Eve, feeling tired.

"You don't need history lessons, Oliver. You can just go back in time and check things out for yourself," she teased.

Clearly, she still didn't believe what had happened. And who could blame her? But I could think of nothing else. I was deep in thought and not paying attention when Ms Redondo tapped the edge of the table.

"Well, Oliver?" she said. "What's the answer?"

I looked up at her blankly. I had no idea what the question was, so how could I give the answer? The whole class burst into laughter, and I felt a blushing embarrassment rising in my face. The redder and hotter my face got, the more the class laughed.

Again, I closed my eyes and my mind switched to the black hole. I willed it to swallow me up. And again, the electric shock tingled through my body.

I looked around. No one was laughing. Everyone was looking at Ms Redondo. "In which year did Australia become a federation?" Ms Redondo asked.

I had gone back in time by five seconds again.

I shot my hand up.

"Yes, Oliver."

"1901," I said.

"Well done."

No one was laughing at me now.

At lunchtime, I told Eve what had happened. Again, she didn't believe me.

"It's true," I pleaded in frustration.

"Prove it," she said.

"How?" That was the problem. How could I prove it?

That afternoon, we walked home together. When we reached the front of my house, I grabbed Eve's arm excitedly.

"I've got it!" I said.

"Got what?"

"Come inside and I'll prove it."

Inside my house, we sat on the couch in the lounge room.

"Well?" Eve said impatiently.

"Think of a number between 1 and 1000," I said.

"Got one," said Eve.

"654," I said.

"No, it was 810."

I immediately closed my eyes, thought of the black hole and felt the tingle.

"Think of a number between 1 and 1000," I said again.

"Got one," said Eve.

"810," I said.

"No way!" said Eve.

I threw my arms into the air.

"Maybe you just got lucky," she said. "Let's try again."

"Okay, but let's make it harder. This time, think of a number between 1 and 1 million."

"Got one," she said.

"93 000," I said.

"No – 387 163."

"Okay. I know the answer now and am going to take us back in time again. If I get the answer right this time, will you believe me?"

Eve nodded.

I took my mind to the black hole again and, a moment later, I went back in time by five seconds.

"This time, think of a number between 1 and 1 million."

"Got one," she said.

"387 163," I said.

Eve threw her arms around me.

"I believe you!" she screamed.

Chapter 7

The Surprise Party

It was great to finally have someone who believed me, but it didn't change things. Eve wasn't able to time travel with me. She couldn't experience what I was experiencing. And it didn't change the fact that Dad still wanted me to fill in the hole. But at least Eve was someone to talk to.

We chatted that afternoon as Eve helped me start to fill the hole. We worked as slowly as we could because I guessed that if the hole was helping me travel, then it made sense that once the hole was gone, there'd be no more time travel.

Dad, though, was keen for the hole to be filled quicker. He came out several times and asked us to hurry it up. He even found another spade for Eve, so we didn't have to take turns resting.

I kept trying to explain the time travel, but he just ignored me. I guess I can't blame him for that. Besides, Mum and Dad had friends coming over for a barbecue on the weekend, and he didn't want anyone accidentally falling into my hole.

But the more we filled in the hole, the more I didn't want it all to end. I had the ability to go back and change things, embarrassing things, even if it was only for five seconds. If we kept going at a slow rate, maybe there'd be at least a few more moments of time travel for me.

The next morning, I was walking to school with Eve when I saw a kid I recognised just ahead – my mate, Hugo. It was his birthday soon, and his mum had invited me to his surprise party. So I raced up to him and tapped him on his shoulder.

He turned.

But it wasn't him. It was a total stranger. And he wasn't looking too happy about being tapped on the shoulder by someone he didn't know.

I heard Eve behind me yell, "Oliver, what are you doing?"

Embarrassment hit hard. I saw the black hole, felt the tingle, and I went back in time.

Except I hadn't gone back five seconds. I only went back about three seconds, which was just enough time to not tap the shoulder of the person who looked like Hugo.

Later that day, as Eve and I slowly – very slowly – continued to fill the hole, I asked her about the person who looked like Hugo. She didn't remember a thing, which again proved I had gone back in time and changed events.

"I reckon it's because the hole's getting smaller," she said, after some deep thought. "It means the time you can go back is becoming shorter."

I reckoned she was right.

And the next day proved it. I was leaving school when I bumped into Hugo. The real Hugo.

"Can't wait for your birthday party this weekend," I said.

He looked at me blankly. He had no idea what I was talking about. Oh, no! I had forgotten it was a surprise party. His mum had told us all to keep it quiet.

Black hole, tingle, back in time. I only went back two seconds. I'd just bumped into Hugo and was about to speak.

"See you tomorrow," I said.

"See you tomorrow," he said back.

Chapter 8

Time Vanishes

That afternoon, Eve and I filled in a little more of the hole. By the time we were called in for dinner, the soil was not quite up to the top. "We'll get it finished tomorrow," I told her.

"No more time travel," said Eve.

"No," I agreed, and felt sad. I might not have gone back to different historical eras and it might only have been a few seconds, but it was fun, and I really didn't want it to end. But, as they say, you can't always have what you want.

"I reckon I'm down to about one second," I told Eve, laughing and pointing to what was left to fill.

"There's not much you can change in just one second," she said.

"I guess not."

Nothing happened at school the next day that I had to go back in time to fix, and I assumed I had been wrong about still having one second of time travel left. But I wasn't wrong. Not only was I not wrong, I was also about to make what could have been the biggest mistake of my life.

On the way home, turning the corner into our street, I playfully nudged Eve's shoulder with mine.

She overbalanced onto the road, right into the path of a truck. No way was it going to miss her.

I closed my eyes and imagined the black hole. I got the tingle.

Opening my eyes, I was just about to give Eve a nudge. But this time I pulled away. She stayed on the footpath and a truck whizzed past. I grabbed Eve's hand just to make sure she was safe.

I started shaking from head to toe.

"What's wrong?" Eve asked.

There was no way I was going to tell her what had happened. Who knows how she'd react?

If we'd filled in the hole yesterday, I wouldn't have been able to go back in time. Not even by a second. That all-important second. If we'd filled in the hole yesterday, she'd ... Best not to think about it.

I remembered what Eve had said: "There's not much you can change in just one second."

She'll never know how wrong she was.

Back home, I wondered whether I should convince Dad to let me keep a little bit of the hole. One second of time travel was better than no seconds of time travel.

But the more I thought about it, the more I realised that it was best to fill the hole. Going back in time meant that I could make mistakes and go back and fix them. But it would be better if I learnt not to make mistakes. I needed to think before I spoke, and to think before I acted. Everyone else had to do that, so why not me?

Eve and I shovelled the last of the earth into the hole, and then smoothed it over. We stood back and admired our handiwork.

Dad came out to inspect.

“Well done,” he said, handing us some drinks. “Took a while,” he added. “But better late than never.” And he went back into the house.

Eve put an arm around me. She knew exactly what I was thinking. My time travel days were over.

That night, I started reading another book. This one had nothing to do with time travel. It was about huge machines: the world's largest tractors and trucks and earth diggers and ...

Earth diggers!

My mind started racing.

When I'm grown up, I could buy a farm and an earth digger. And I could dig a hole, a massive hole, the largest black hole ever dug. And maybe, just maybe ...